UNQUIET STARS

UNQUIET STARS

Ann K. Schwader

Trade Paperback Edition

Editor, F. J. Bergmann
Editor & Publisher, Joe Morey

ISBN: 978-1-888993-47-9

Book design by F. J. Bergmann

Weird House Press
Central Point, OR 97502
www.weirdhousepress.com

For Linda

Also by Ann K Schwader

Dark Energies (P'rea Press, 2015)

Twisted in Dream: the Collected Weird Poetry of Ann K. Schwader (Hippocampus Press, 2011)

Wild Hunt of the Stars (Sam's Dot, 2010)

In the Yaddith Time (Mythos Books, 2007)

Architectures of Night (Dark Regions, 2003)

The Worms Remember (Hive Press, 2001)

The Weird Sonneteers (with Keith Allen Daniels and Jerry H. Jenkins; Anamnesis Press, 2000)

Werewoman (Nocturnal Publications, 1990)

Table of Contents

Star-Tide

The stars have turned already. Now the tides
are following, devouring all light
& land alike into that liquid night
we drew our first breaths fearing. No divide
remains for us: our levees, dikes, & pride
lie shattered under glaciers' final flight
from ice to ocean, savaged by the bite
of calculations fatally denied.

Small island nations perish swiftly, spared
the weight of waiting. We who cling to cliffs
of concrete canyons dream ourselves destroyed
by what those tides reveal: a war declared
& lost long aeons since. Like hieroglyphs
of flesh, our rising masters hail the void.

The Language of Forgotten Gods

The language of forgotten gods is not
so far from ours—no farther than a curse
our spirits harbor, though our flesh forgot.

Epigraphers (without a second thought)
transcribe from temple ruins, verse by verse,
the language of forgotten gods. Is not

pale summary enough? Perhaps they sought
enlightenment. . . . Or something more perverse.
Our spirits harbor—though our flesh forgot—

persistent echoes of some cosmic plot
against this planet. Better to be terse:
the language of forgotten gods is not

for amateurs, & even experts ought
to watch their glottal stops. There's no reverse
our spirits harbor, though our flesh forgot

what agonies such overlords allot
to ignorance. And next time may be worse.
The language of forgotten gods is not
our spirits' harbor, though our flesh forgot.

Final Library

A palimpsest repurposed from some past
lost manuscript—*well lost*—its surface shone
illuminated. Sacred writings vast
& vacant with ape-faith had overgrown
that void once offered to a Voice unknown
by any mortal name. Yet what it spoke
still echoed there to summon shadows flown
from darker stars than ours, & worlds that broke
beneath their wings.
                                        Indelible, they soaked
through layered ignorance to snare the gaze
of some wise idiot—who then uncloaked
each syllable, each fatal turn of phrase,
& called it scholarship. The sky outside
cracked black with nightmares as our last hope died.

Under the Plumed Serpent's Temple

With a bulb twist, dusk. Pyrite ignites galaxies on walls already receding to dream. Constellations pulse new myths against his mind. Heartbeat of the People. Cadence of emergence. Forty feet underground under open sky, the archaeologist staggers. Shadow coils tighten his chest. Fragile shattering.

These are not his stars. There is no way home.

fingerprints
on the outside
night pane

The Moon-Gate

Set into some forgotten garden wall
between two desolations, it defies
the curious with cryptic glyphs that rise
& shimmer into twilight. Hardly tall
enough for use, its lunar curve betrays
no age or origin—the very stone
contributing a riddle of its own
in fossil traces faint as spectral haze.

Stout chains are strung at sunset to deny
all possibility of passage to
oblivion. On nights when only stars
illuminate our firmament, the sky
inside reveals a weirdly silvered view:
the moon this gate encloses is not ours.

Children of the Stone

We have not always been this planet's masters,
though humankind denies it. Other blood
than ours heaped earthen barrows, raised up stones
in veneration of some dark & nameless
power, avatar of elder shadow
slithered through the star-rifts. What survives

is myth & madness. Whispers that survive
the rise of tribes still struggling to master
fire's miracle speak only of those shadows
that dawn dispels, yet cannot silence blood
deep knowledge of another. Gripped by nameless
apprehension, some adore a stone

like Void incarnate. When it thirsts, their stone
war-mallets spatter tribute. Few survive
to view the aftermath: a trail of nameless
hieroglyphs disclosed by gore. Unmastered
by any of their prehistoric blood,
this text recedes once more into the shadows

for centuries—until some unclean shadow
congeals to godhead, squatting on that stone
where rituals of torment, fear, & blood
have finally summoned what should not survive
beneath a wholesome sky to overmaster
its votaries. They call it by a name less

word than sibilance: a kind of nameless
invocation, serpentine & shadowed
as that inscription. By strange dreams, they master
each tainted incantation, drench the stone
in what its demon craves. No tribe survives
their rising, until heroes born to blood—

bold Gael or Briton, Pict or Saxon— blood
their bronze & iron blades among these nameless
changelings. Only stragglers survive
within the sanctuary of deep-shadowed
tunnels torn like wounds through living stone,
devolved & mutant mirrors of their master.

Yet it is said that blood spilled in the shadows
of nameless dolmens may call forth that stone's
true servants who survive . . . or their dread master.

Salisbury Twilight

The shades of ancient dynasties remain
past sunset as the last midwinter light
scrawls shadow artifacts across this plain.

In life they left no writing to explain
these stones they raised for nameless gods' delight:
the shades of ancient dynasties remain

mysterious as potsherds. Why profane
such sacred ignorance? A blade of night
scrawls shadow artifacts across this plain

& graceless landscape, granting even rain
some incantation all its own. So might
the shades of ancient dynasties remain,

as whispers grown too muted for mundane
perception. Nothing mortal (or not quite)
scrawls shadow artifacts. Across this plain

where one sun dies & one is born again,
survivals such as these seem strangely right.
The shades of ancient dynasties remain
scrawls. Shadow artifacts across this plain.

Deep Winter Skies

There is no comfort in such clarity,
So many stellar mysteries unveiled
To wary eyes as singularity
Shifts onward into ominous. What pale
& faceless specter haunts the Hyads? Failed
Carcosa flickers out beneath black stars
Somewhere in Taurus, while dark wisdom's trail
Twists through the Pleiades. Osiris, scarred
By death & yet undying rises far
Above the Western tombs, his belt alight
To guide the justified—although there are
None left to follow through abyssal night,
Or sense beyond it, blind & unaware,
Some vast intelligence that does not care.

Distant Deaths of Galaxies

The distant deaths of galaxies
disturb the surface of our sleep,
disclosing cataclysms deep
& yet familiar. All of these
sad spirals with their energies
stripped off by darkness warn us: keep
what's sacred secret. Safe. No cheap
diversions, shadow dives to ease
the pangs of starbirth. Soon enough
& few enough, our final sparks
cool into void, rejoining dreams
this universe abandoned. Snuffed
husks linger like graffiti marked
on rocks that cross a lightless stream.

The Dark Reclaims Us

The dark reclaims us one by one
Within her arms, against our wills,
Unnatural children of the sun.

Reluctant to admit we're done,
We stay out late, our voices shrill
As dark reclaims us. One by one,

Doors open. Close again. What fun
Is this? Alone now, growing chilled,
Unnatural children of the sun

Without our star. This year's undone
& flapping in the branches—still
The dark reclaims us one by one

To primal silence. Sparing none,
She wraps us tight. Our time fulfilled,
Unnatural children of the sun

Drift deeper into sleep begun
With autumn & the blood it spilled
While dark reclaims us one by one,
Unnatural children of the sun.

Apocalypse Swap

Apocalypse was simple once. A phone
the shade of midnight sunrise rang somewhere
in Washington or Moscow, & the moan

of missiles filled our momentary air
to bursting with their urgency. One flash
before the sirens' silence—then, who cared

what happened next? We fixed our hopes on ash
& shadows, all the madness burned away
forever. Now we watch a planet trashed

& drowning in Antarctica's decay
depopulate—too slowly—in its shroud
of satellites. How many years afraid

before whatever exit we've endowed
our future with? I miss that mushroom cloud.

New World Haunting

Sleep capsules failed: we never found out why
our rest became eternal. All in all,
you couldn't ask a finer way to die,

aside from not quite knowing. Planetfall
unlatched our clamshells. Thawing into dust
& spirit, we persisted, though the call

to disembark rang hollow as the trust
we'd wired our lives into. Against a sun
that spawns no shadows, drifting as we must

across this landscape loaded like a gun
no longer fit to kill us, we aspire
despite ourselves. Or lack of same. Undone

in flesh, we colonize by raw desire
a fellow wanderer through distant fires.

Ghost Dunes

Ghost dunes, the xeno-geos named
these crescent scars that Martian sand
carved in its passing. Wind proclaimed
its lost direction on the land
in pitted arrowheads like hands
now pointing nowhere, titans blown
to dust. Though scientists demand
no more of ghosts, this haunting sown
in isolated minds has grown
prodigiously. When evening spills
across plateaus here, some unknown
frisson soon rises to a chill
like recognition at first sight
of red dune riders in the night.

Stone Ghosts

for the drought cult caves, Belize

Drop by drop, our shrouds accrete beneath
the storms that came too late to save us. Here
beside these lightless rivers underground
we left our years.

If men are maize & even gods must eat,
the tenderest should please them best. Too young
for fieldwork or the fruitless hunt, we fell
on unseen tongues.

Each tear a prayer, our invocations flowed
in tribute to the fickle names of rain:
Chac & Tlaloc & all nameless ones
who savor pain.

Like jars our elders filled below pale fangs
still dripping with the gift of distant skies,
we poured our hearts' libations to the last,
& then we died.

Those gods are lost to silence now. Despite
our sacrifice, we linger here alone
& dry inside this bitter glittering,
small ghosts of stone.

The Dead in Spring

The dead in spring go whispering beneath
each wind that lends a blossom motion. Time
betrays us to their voices, calm & kind
& final as a frost in April. *Dream*
this greening if it pleases you, but see
how fast it fades to fruit, the fruit to nights
of crickets silenced . . . year by year, they sigh
away this season from our blood. The peace
they leave us is less memory than stone
already chiseled with a stranger's name
& left to mark our passing. All we are
drifts into petals scattering below
these futile branches scented with their strange
sweet promise of the worm within our hearts.

The Final Turn

The story at its start is innocent
enough: a governess, a pair of children
sequestered in the countryside where secrets
root deepest. Throw in rumors of a death
or two, an honest housekeeper still haunted
by something subtle. Shadows of the damned

begin their flickering at windows, damned
anew by hope. Such flawless innocent
young vessels fairly cry out to be haunted,
yet none suspect how quickly. Why should children
so sheltered, so protected offer death
a set of playthings? *Surely nursery secrets*

suffice. Too soon for twilight with its secret
anticipations . . . assignations . . . damned
& damning consequences. Let the death
of candor come to other innocents,
but spare these two: so guardians, like children
themselves, weave fantasies against the haunted

inevitable dark. Where lives are haunted
by silence, these conspiracies of secrets
may pass unnoticed. Only ghosts & children
slip through illusion, choosing to be damned
instead by truth, the brutal innocence
of what cannot be changed. Presuming death

is silent also, that no tongue of death
might find a living speaker leaves the haunted

adrift within themselves, too innocent
to know their own corruption. Keeping secrets
becomes a creeping habit, no less damned
for being charming—charming as these children

worn now as masks by phantoms playing children
against approaching autumn, flaunting death
from every windowpane & tower. Damned
as disbelievers, fragile allies haunted
in every sense must resurrect the secret,
deny the obvious. The innocent.

And with the dawn, these shells of children haunted
by selfish death surrender every secret,
leaving survivors damned by innocence.

—after Henry James' *The Turn of the Screw*

Snatching Shadows

Was the poet John Keats a graverobber?
—*BBC Culture* article, 7/23/19

The dead lack poetry. No Grecian ode
enlivens those who slumber—briefly—down
in potter's field until their flesh & bones
emerge as guineas. Torn from humble ground
to serve once more, such silent nightingales
as these inspire no listeners to mark
their passage into shadow. Yet each page
confesses otherwise: in language drawn
from certain moonless & secluded work
amid grief's ruins, mortal longing shades
to soil disrupted. Ashes scattered. Turn
suspicion elsewhere, reader. Do not name
this surgical precision of design,
the midnight science whispered in his rhymes.

Tomb-Feasters

They hunt in packs of shadow, Ammut's blood
Made manifest in every nightmare face
The moon refuses. Hunger like a flood
Suffuses them, reducing sacred space
To chaos. Silence. Hieroglyphs erased
By claws or jaws no longer guide the dead
Along their western roads, while hearts replaced
By emptied jars turn merciless. Unread,
Their witness tips Thoth's scale, reveals that dread
Called *second death*—& for the merest taste
Of natron-seasoned flesh, a soul instead
Meets entropy incarnate. Laid to waste,
Another tomb reveals—*for those who see*—
The leavings of a lost eternity.

Blue Suns

Morning glory seeds are tough enough for an interplanetary trip.
—Science

Starship. Ribcage. Trellis. Dawn on this wrong world turns them equal, twisted thick with vines too fragile to survive us. Though they have. Rad-fried stillbirths, cold sleep cinderlings, we stare skullblind into brief blue suns.

comet's tail
under how many skies
one garden

A City Built On Bones

A city built on bones cannot deny
its origins: the skull racks & the blood,
the ones who perished never knowing why.

Cathedrals painting faith across the sky
arose from altars to some darker god
a city built on bones cannot deny,

but only bury. Briefly. As the cries
of earthquake sacrifices fade to mud,
the ones who perished never knowing why

embrace them. Heartless, flayed, & shadow-eyed,
they claim their kin at once. Is this so odd?
A city built on bones cannot deny

its native citizens. Although the lies
of men, not gods, unleashed this sanguine flood,
the ones who perished never knowing why

are no less dead, their lives torn out to buy
the sun back. Haunted legacy of fraud,
a city built on bones cannot deny
the ones who perished never knowing why.

Temple of the Plumed Serpent

—Teotihuacán (Nahuatl): the place where men become gods

How men became gods here, or where they went,
abandoning this land for stranger skies
whose myths are sanguine miracles, defies
our scholarship. Although their monuments
depict a grim & oceanic birth,
titanic serpents, jaguars . . . all life
that means us death, we symbolize the knife
against our throats until it shatters. Earth
served only as their merest shadow-stage,
where dramas darker, deeper than our time
upon this rock replayed to realign
our destiny.
                    What cruel future age
of servitude awaits us may be read
in glyphs of pyrite swirling far beneath
our feet. Inside that tunnel's subtle glow,
a galaxy expands—its center dead
within a drift of mysteries, a wreath
unlike the constellations that we know.

Faces From the House of Pain

after *The Island of Dr. Moreau*
by H. G. Wells

I. The Face At the Rail

His silhouette against the clotted stars
of midnight over open ocean gave
no indication of its strangeness, save
for silence. I returned to my cigar
without a thought—until one backward glance
transfixed me. Phosphorescent, pallid green
as absinthe, nothing human in its mien
compelled my fellow feeling. What mischance
connected us? As childhood terrors rose
from memory's abyss to stalk my mind
afresh, I took a breath . . . & felt that stream
of madness falter. Fail. What I'd supposed
seemed distant as the starlight left behind
when I retired to my unquiet dreams.

II. The Face In the Laboratory

While suffering is silent, it remains
invisible—yet torment giving tongue
is eloquent with nightmare, each nerve wrung
beyond endurance. Certain that the pain
I heard was human, I abandoned all
the cautions my hosts caged me with, & crossed
from innocence to one forever lost
in bitter knowing. As I stood appalled
& staring past that too-unguarded door
that gaped upon damnation, something bound
upon a framework shrieked its agony
both female & feline. A moment more
sufficed to rout me, heedless of the sound
of shackles rattling. Wrenching. Working free.

III. The Face of the Law

A refugee from science, I arrived
among the ones I feared I might become,
& found rough welcome there. Exhausted, numb
to higher thought, fit merely to survive,
I squatted in their darkness till a voice
began the Law. A voice without a face
beyond gray absence, eyes & mouth replaced
alike by shadow, it allowed no choice
save litany: the learning of a slave
who dreads his master's hand. Yet as I swayed
in rhythm with the rest, that fetid den
transfigured into temple for one brave
mad moment. Prophets all, the Law remade
us justified at last. *Were we not Men?*

IV. The Face of the Maker

The pallid certainty of his regard
reduced me to confusion nearing shame
as he disclosed his motives, & proclaimed
my own as futile. Nature makes those hard
who study hardest: stranger to remorse,
evolved past pain, he seemed a thing apart
from beast & man alike; his sanguine art
a species of transfiguration. Forced
at last against obsession's edge, I caught
my breath & listened, hemorrhaging doubt
into the dark around us. Was this skill,
or wickedness akin to godhood? Not
for me to say—a castaway without
the scalpel, whip, & pistol of his will.

V. The Face In the Forest

Let none escape who break the Law! That horde
before us howled approval, & arose
at once to run their own to ground. In throes
of bloodlust justice, craving no reward
beyond the moment's slaughter, they—& I
unwilling with them—hunted one who dared
distain Moreau's largesse, its twisted snare
slipped past redemption. With a leopard's cry,
he claimed himself again, all emerald rage
& four-foot cunning. Balanced on the brink
of breaking, staring down the House of Pain's
perverse plasticity, his soul engaged
some fragment of my own. Some last instinct
that put a bullet's mercy through his brain.

VI. The Faces of Catastrophe

We found them dead together, in the end,
creator & creation each unmade
in one red moment. Had the maker's blade
betrayed its wielder? Helpless to defend
against the broken fetters that secured
his masterwork in progress—& in hell—
Moreau lay maimed & battered where he fell
as sacrifice to her who had endured
his last ambition. Children of the Law
no longer, lost & bloodied by a fruit
too long forbidden, gorged themselves on death
that afternoon. Returning with him raw
as his materials, our last tribute
destroyed all that remained of pain & breath.

VII. The Faces of Exile

I heard their voices hollow in the night,
two exiles severed utterly from all
their former joys & sorrows by the call
of knowledge. Fallen headlong from that height
he loved as London, one dissolved regret
into distilled oblivion; one fled
a butchered heritage to make his bed
in no man's land, yet some instinctual threat
connected them. Their ending when it came
was swift & savage: senseless as the beasts
one rose from, one descended to. They lay
among the ashes of a hope unnamed
until impossible. Both found release—
but which died as a man, I could not say.

VIII. The Face of the Last Friend

I laid me down the last of all my kind
upon that blighted island, barely more
than one among its creatures. Yet before
I fully woke to my demotion, blind
with pride, another came & would not leave
my ravaged life. Familiar as the cave
deep chronicle of man & canine—brave
past self-regard—I watched but scarcely grieved
as he resumed his truth. Moreau improved
so little, marred so greatly: innocent
once more, my only comrade held the dark
at bay until it found his throat. Thus moved
by grief, I rediscovered some intent
to live two-footed. Leave a human mark.

IX. The Face In the Mirror

The outward is not all, nor even most
of our humanity. Though London streets
are crowded thick with men, each one repeats
in form or carriage something of that host
I fled as bestial; barely half-wrought souls
already failing. Driven from their midst
by my own chronic terror, I exist
in solitude. Wise books for self-control,
& wiser stars for guardians: such things
are touchstones now against the stubborn flesh
that threatens this reflection. To deny
my near escape is futile. Nightfall brings
the Law's nadir in memories refreshed
behind the feral brightness of my eyes.

All Masks are Mirrors

All masks are mirrors in the end:
Reflections of some inward scar,
Some pallid truth that we defend.

Beneath black stars, our dreams portend
No future tense. Why seek so far?
All masks are mirrors in the end,

& cracked at that. As cloud-waves blend
Our souls with night, some avatar
Of pallid truth that we defend

Awakes at last. Unmasks. Extends
Its curse to hurl against the stars:
All masks are mirrors. In the end,

Carcosa claims us all, my friend;
Past time for bidding au revoir
To pallid truth. That we defend

This specter of our lost lives lends
A certain melancholy—are
All masks but mirrors, in the end?
Some pallid truth that we defend?

Corridors Enough

The brain has corridors enough
To host a hundred ghosts of selves
Outgrown, outlasted, or rebuffed.
The brain has corridors enough,
But doors & windows? Missing. Tough
To exorcise such bitter elves:
The brain has corridors enough
To host a hundred ghosts of selves.

—after Dickinson

Volunteers

Springtime is no time for the dead, & yet
they rise unbidden like any other
perennial. Scented with recollection,
their pallid buds emerge at midnight
in the mind & open slowly
as voices fading. As words regretted
they spread against the moon, each petal
loves me not or loved too late
for more than shadow. Less than cloud
between that cold reflected light
& eyes denied to sleep, their bloom
obscures the certainty of stars
we thought to wish on. To turn back
by will alone one season's haunting.

In SETI Silence

The Drake Equation failed us. Once we thought
belief might be enough: just listen hard
& cross your fingers. Easy. We forgot

how fragile intellect gets, battle-scarred
by every little cataclysm. Let
a war or three go really wrong; the charred

remains sulk into silence, blood & sweat
& tears alike rejoining void. That pond
should still be full of signal-ripples—yet

somehow it's not. Turns out the stars beyond
are haunted only sparsely. Holding on
until we notice (let alone respond)

asks far too much of people eons gone,
their planets cracked to dust or blown to red
irradiated vapor. Science spawned

a guesstimate to clutter up our heads
with saucer saviors. Don't be comforted:
we're on our own. The aliens are dead.

Dark Hearts

The shadow of this galaxy's dark heart
eludes our instruments. No siren jet
reveals itself in radio to mark
annihilation's border, or befriend
our fatal curiosity. Except
for hunches, we have nothing: faith alone
disclosed the beast, & faith alone compels
a fragile global net of telescopes
we set to catch horizon's whisper. Known
by intuition only, it persists
as evidence—or echo—of our souls'
lost source in stardeath. Lacking origins
beyond biology, we crave this maw
that gapes upon the void inside us all.

The Vestals

By day they pass in silence through the streets
of Empire, spotless mantles wrapped up tight
Against their throats. No dust upon these feet!
No sweat on any brow—no thoughts save white
Fire leaping on the altar of the home
Incarnate: Vesta, hearth & heart of Rome.

Yet deep in urban darkness with the moon
Their only witness, certain shadows run
Unmantled. Neither lictor nor tribune
Encompasses their law, & no man's son
Dares meet the incandescence of these eyes
Bereft of daylight's maidenly disguise.

Milk sisters to the founders of this state
Which raised itself with steel & blood, they claim
Their heritage in flesh: the slave, the great,
Invader, traitor . . . any Jove might name
Unworthy of survival fall beneath
The fury of their judgment. And their teeth.

Did Numitor's wronged daughter comprehend
What mysteries a lunar vow might wake
Within her blood? No matter. In the end,
A king's fall & a brother's death must make
Unwilling consecration second to
Those tactics that the Twelve alone pursue.

Just such awaited her that night she fled
Great Vesta's sanctuary for a place
Raw as her raging spirit. Nearly dead
With grief, she wandered past the farthest trace
Of man's betrayal—yet within that wild,
She met a god instead, & left with child.

Nine months beyond, her temple's endless flame
Flickered & failed. Twin cries disturbed the peace
Of Alba's false inheritor: though shame
Condemned her to a living death, his niece
Regretted nothing. *Sons of Mars,* she said,
That's who I've borne. Go tell it to the dead.

By sunset, she was underground, entombed
With bread & light & little else to smooth
Her passing into Pluto's realm. Presumed
Well on her way, she waited for the truth
Of moonrise—& the beast that she'd embraced—
To fire her heart & tear her from that place.

Soon only rags of carrion remained
To mark the minions set to guard her death,
Yet frenzy drove her on. Milk-heavy, pained
Past circumstance, she searched the length & breadth
Of Alba's territory for those two
She'd given all to work her vengeance through.

Meanwhile, the task of killing children fell
On one who loved the law before his king.
Trusting his charges to the Tiber's swell,
He prayed some river-deity might bring
Their cradle safely home . . . & in the trees,
A she-wolf whimpered at a telltale breeze.

The rest is history. Or myth. Or some
Of both, inscribed in tyrant blood that night
A war god's whelps restored their grandsire from
Disgraceful exile. Blinking in the light
Still silvering his victory, he sighed
For their lost mother & the way she'd died.

The name of Rhea Silvia is dust.
The fame of Lupa, tainted by men's fears—
But in the eyes of some who keep the trust
Of Vesta's hearth, a hybrid flame appears:
The woman in the wolf, the wolf in she
Whose blood reclaims the night's ferocity.

The Thirst of Sekhmet

There is a crying on this twilight wind
Like some great lioness who scents the blood
Of Aegypt spilled afresh: that primal flood
Re once unleashed. Just how the people sinned
Against their god is lost, but his reply
Clawed swift in hieroglyphs of solar fire
Across men's hearts, translating his desire
For retribution through his daughter. Eye
Of vengeance merciless as midday heat,
She hunted & she slaughtered & she bled
Fresh sacrifice enough to wade in red,
Until Re formulated her retreat.

All this is myth; yet myths may still awake
When offered what they crave. The taste of fear
Is salt & copper, spreading like a stain
Across the ravaged land once more to slake
Its first & fiercest rage . . . for it was here
A goddess thirsted. And shall thirst again.

Sepulcher of Saints

Death carries no corruption for the pure
among us, stainless souls who went to rest
in innocence & youth, salvation sure

as their entombed expressions all attest
unblushing. Maidens pale as winter light,
they seem to sleep, hands folded on their breasts

in holy meditation. Pilgrims might
abandon time here. Captured by the awe
of beauty proof against eternal night,

some linger after twilight's warning, draw
too close. As lips no longer chastely sealed
against temptation part—revealing raw

reality writ sharp—these seekers feel
themselves delivered. Kiss by savored kiss
of peace, our saints sustain themselves to heal

this dying world, transfiguring in bliss
some few elect. Lest ignorance betray
itself, the ones unlikely to be missed

are chosen first. Yet everyone must pray
unceasingly to be among the brave
who stay behind, & speed that moonlit day

when we shall all be saints together: saved
beyond redemption, rising from our graves.

Midnight in the Hot Zone

Our tribe is virus. Blood by blood we spread
A hunger like contagion in the vein,
Sharp-kindled & insatiable. Undead,
Our tribe is virus. Blood by blood we spread
These vacant mirrors of ourselves ahead
Through centuries. Mere witnesses to pain,
Our tribe is virus. Blood by blood we spread
A hunger like contagion in the vein.

Temple of the Condor

(Machu Picchu)

No mere formation, but the outstretched wings
of something neither stone nor sky might birth,
the shadows that it casts upon this place
are not of Earth.

Men named it condor for its sacred scar
of darkness drawn across that upper world
where sun & moon & lightning & the stars
turn gods unfurled.

Beneath these fearsome pinions they incised
the rest in arabesques of head & beak,
suggestions of some elder entity
no tongue may speak.

Less art than abattoir, those channels cut
in replication of a raptor's might
permitted liquid sacrifice to drain
down into night.

What thirsted to receive it there remains
a source of mystery: few tourists dare
that lightless cavern guides deny, & seek
more wholesome air.

Yet when Andean mists obscure the trail
that winds to safety, wanderers & fools
still scramble through. The consequences spread
in sanguine pools.

Goldilocks Stars

We speculate from desperation born
of knowledge we must not acknowledge. Chained
by ignorance to this one crowded, worn
& aging sphere, our destiny is plain
as fossil prints. Yet something in the brains
of *Homo sapiens* denies this night,
however universal. What remains
beyond it? Stars—& maybe one just right
to kindle sparks like ours. A kinder light
with longer lifespan, not too hot or cold
for children in the wilderness who might
forget grim stories nobody gets told
these days, & gorge on porridge, unaware
there are no hosts here. Only hungry bears.

Solving For X

So now our wise astronomers deny
a need for Planet X. Whatever force
is pulling distant planetoids off-course
need not be singular & shadowed. Why,
an orbiting of icy pebbles might
suffice as well. Less drama & less fuss
means sounder science, separating us
from morbid fascination with some night
beyond our logic. Only dreams insist
upon a whisper of crustacean wings
above the Yuggoth hives—& what they bring
in certain strange containers that resist
all waking understanding, as they keep
the weight of nightmare tugging at our sleep.

Stranger Tides

Our science speaks of waves we cannot see,
the artifacts of some titanic chance
event: leviathans locked in a dance
that ripples space-time. Roiling gravity
is silent as a scream in vacuum, yet
such waves may be translated into song
cetacean, ominous, & hollow. Long
before it fades out, most of us forget
translation is not truth. Nor eyes to part
the void, & witness for ourselves what sings
disruption through our universe—or wrings
reality until things rip apart.

It falls to dreamers in their fevered nights
beyond the reach of science to perceive
what light & time conceal. What shadowed forms
we have no names for, only myths that warn
against the innocent who still believe
that knowledge equals wisdom equals light.

Lightless Oceans

The lightless oceans of our nightmares hold
a thousand shadows. Shaped by legends lost
to time or science, writhing in their cold
& utter void, they touch our minds with frost
past waking's warming. Yet this holocaust
of strange imagination fades away
before seas comprehended. Conquered. Crossed
off every list of myths—until one day
some minor moonlet cracks its crust, betrays
us into darkness. Far beneath that ice
flows living liquid, although life displays
no hint of the familiar here. Precise
as any apex nightmare, it awaits
our tardy understanding of man's fate.

Toward Samhain

The dead are patient on their side.
Like fallen leaves, they murmur through
That mist between upon the tide
Of summer's failing breath, pursue
Forgotten pleasures, & delay
Their crossing for some future day.

The dead are watching on their side.
Though ravens cry in welcome raw
& unmistakable to guide
Such wanderers, the year-wheel's law
Decrees another sun must burn
To ash & night for their return.

The dead are restless on their side.
As twilight creeps toward afternoon,
They mingle with those shadows, hide
Themselves within the dusk . . . for soon
That veil which parts two worlds must part
Before the silence of their hearts.

The dead are hungry on their side.
Bereft of mortal warmth & light
Too long already, they abide
Upon our doorsteps; or invite
Themselves inside to fill their plates
With fading love, & hoarded hate.

Pink Crosses

(Ciudad Juàrez)

This field grows ghosts. So many seeds,
so thickly planted, must in turn
produce a bumper crop that bleeds.

What phantoms fester when men's needs
negate the law? Not hard to learn:
this field grows ghosts (so many?), seeds

the wind with whispering that feeds
a woman's fears. Yet girls must earn,
produce. A bumper crop that bleeds

means little as their shift proceeds
homeward by night. Not all return;
this field grows. Ghosts, so many seeds

of futures stillborn, spring like weeds
from midnight gravesites. Such nocturnes
produce a bumper crop that bleeds

between these silences that breed
a deeper silence, less concern.
This field grows ghosts. So many seeds
produce a bumper crop that bleeds.

Two Meetings

You seized us meeting in the wood,
& swore we met the Devil there,
A dozen witches & their lord.
You saw the Devil everywhere,

As godly men are wont to do
When God & law are linked as one.
Surrounded, bound, & locked away,
We understood our lives were done

For being old & destitute,
Or maidens marred by their own minds
Too often spoken. Sacred tests
Performed as they had been designed,

Condemning all. From your high seat,
Predestination tolled our fate
As holy writ: undone from birth,
We twelve should not be made to wait,

But join our master in his place
Upon the morrow. Neighbors stared
As if at strangers. Not the wise
Who met to gather herbs, prepared

Such simples & such charms as might
Turn back the darkness from their lives . . .
No longer. Bleating piously,
They drove their daughters & their wives

Away from us who at first light
Shall feast the crows on Gallows Hill,
While you at leisure rise to greet
The Devil in your mirror still.

A Wizard's Daughter

for Asenath, at last

A wizard's daughter is a foredoomed child.
Denied the recognition of her sire
whose vision cannot scry beyond the form
of female, she must magnify her will
while passing for a mirror of his wisdom
solely. Innocent of mother-blood

to all appearances, she mingles blood
with ink, begins her training as the child
of shadows manifest. Forbidden wisdom
comes easiest: the birth-gift of a sire
ensnared by something Other, ageless will
still interwoven with this aged form

of flesh now fading. Failing. Nature forms
the surest remedy, though even blood
is not enough to satisfy him. Will
some fragile wickerwork of woman-child
suffice a mind like his? He'd thought to sire
an heir as reliquary for dark wisdom

worked upon the world. A long life's wisdom
cannot compress itself so; surely form
corrupts its function. Far too late to sire
another: he must make the most of blood
blighted by strange bargaining. This child
is his alone, last testament & will

bequeathed to no one— yet her infant will
resists. Delivered by a mother's wisdom
both alien & unsuspected, child
no longer, it assumes its proper form
at last. Begins its thirsting for the blood
of her usurper. Turned aside, her sire

seduced by Otherness (that primal sire
of myth & madness) hesitates. Whose will
is this? What hybrid spirit fills this blood
& flesh he meant as vessel? Lacking wisdom
not found in books, he only sees the form
before him. Never thinks *her mother's child.*

Betrayed at first by blood, & now by wisdom
overthrown, the dying sire finds will
prevails in many forms. One was his child.

. . . she was Ephraim Waite's daughter—the child of his old age by an unknown wife who always went veiled.
—H. P. Lovecraft, "The Thing on the Doorstep"

The City in the Sands

Because they understood no gods but theirs,
& cut themselves adrift from history,
A pack of ragged jackals made their lair
Among half-buried ruins, unaware
They trespassed in the realm of mysteries.

No hand of man raised up the nameless stones
That formed this place. No human thought conceived
Its guardians—for we are not alone,
& never have been through the eons flown
Since void-spawned terrors taught our world to grieve.

The jackals with their ropes & hammers broke
Each image of those guardians to shards
& shattered shadows. *Heresy,* they spoke
In undertones, unwilling to provoke
The twilight creeping softly. Falling hard.

They kindled watch-fires in the city streets,
Sustaining them on scavenged texts whose tongues
Were old before Irem . . . & yet no heat
Arose from so much burning to defeat
A depth of desert chill that bit & stung.

At last a bitter gust of wind arose
That sent a thousand shadows clawing high
In spectral vengeance as their victims froze,
Acknowledging in vain the shapes of those
Lost guardians now blotting out the sky.

Bereft of men & gods alike, these walls
Lie silent in the selfsame dawn that shone
On Sarnath & Mnar. Here too the call
Of history rang clearly over all
This shifting sand that whispers over bones.

Last Justice

Eternity is not for all. Dark hearts
That drop against Truth's feather shall be cast
Away from green deliverance. The vast
Amnesia of the desert—every part
Reduced to silent dust—will not suffice
For *Isfet's* minions. Proven false of voice
Upon Thoth's scale, a worse & certain choice
Remains: the namelessness of dying twice.

Past sunset, when unwholesome shadows seep
From ruined tombs to howl at temple gates
With hunger more than mortal, priests await
These avatars of Ammut—though they keep
Their faces well averted from that feast
None speak of. None who long for life, at least.

Haunted Innsmouth

Some subtle presence permeates these streets
Scant sunlight touches. Shadows seep between
Cross-boarded windows, reaching out with lean
& spectral fingertips as if to greet
Unwary strangers. Wraiths of mist retreat
From closer observation, never seen
For long or well enough . . . although unclean
Suspicion whispers of the worm's defeat.

No spirit lingers here, but flesh made strange
Through dealings with the deep. All those who thrive
By such abyssal rites shall never die
Except by violence—nor live unchanged
In open air. So Obed's kin survive
As timeless exiles, shuttered from the sky.

Mercurial Musings

Deprived of daylight by their planet's tilt
Or lack of same, deep polar craters lie
In frozen shadow, sheltering the spilt
Remains of asteroids. Though when & why
Such wanderers brought ancient H_2O
Is mystery enough for mortals, *where*
Appears the answer we most need to know,
Or else the catalyst of our despair.

Not every random rock that rattles through
This system hails from here. The outer dark
Holds horrors at its heart—& should a few
Seek breathing space, what safer place to park
Than at some sunless pole? Beneath that ice,
They dream of Their return. Our sacrifice.

Death Spiral, Korolev Crater

Shaved stardust kiss against her faceplate. Perfect backward outside edge. Millimeters above trapped atmosphere, clutching the dead hand of physics, she orbits her partner in this unwinding dream. Ice is water is life but the rads add up. Tosol their relief crew is three hundred twenty sols late.

One point two miles below the rim. Nowhere left to go but around.

almost forgetting their names two moons

Past Equinox

We fallen angels of a failing light
have watched the balance shift against this sky
our wings aspired to. With ascendant night,
we fallen angels of a failing light
revisit once again the strange delights
of destiny. No need to question why:
we fallen angels of a failing light
have watched the balance shift against this sky.

Victrola (At the End of the World)

No power, now, & yet this music holds
a power all its own against the dark
that seeps between these bitter stars & marks
us out as prey forever. Thin & cold
as coyotes in our concrete myth, we fold
each note within a memory, embark
on our investigation unremarked
by any save our furtive footfalls. Old
beyond machines we trusted once to keep
our culture safe, some simple box & horn
is scratching out its foxtrots. Do we dare
reveal the hand that turns it—& our sleep—
to something sacred, something less forlorn
than silence? Do we seek our own despair?

Entropic

Let us leave the rose to the worm, & the cities to vermin.
Let us suffer the mad to enact cataclysms of faith
in the name of whatever void they imagine listens,
while we withdraw to some forgotten island
& cry to the fleeing stars that we are ready.

Our constellations have abandoned us
to white noise & the cataracts of light
that foul our vision outward. No more heroes—
we live behind our eyelids now, forgetting
a little more each day the myth we were.

Snagged by the undertow of reason's redshift,
we struggle less, sleep more. No moon disturbs us
with footfalls lost to history: amnesia
lies trackless as this scrap of beach we wander
& cry to the fleeing stars that we are ready.

O we are ready,
we have been ready
for a long time.

Missed Horizons

Scant hours after nine-plus years. That's all
the time & treasure humankind could spare
to catch a glimpse of secrets seething there
at our creation's rim. If fungi crawl
across that pallid heart—unfurl their wings
in hydrocarbon haze—we may not know
for months. The data's streaming far too slow,
in packets yet to be unpacked. Dark things
deny themselves to science: no device
unaided by imagination knows
enough of Outside perils to expose
inhabitants beneath exotic ice.

Our calculations left too little space
for speculation past the most mundane
details of speed & fuel. With our brains
bewitched at this exhilarating pace,
distracted by fresh baubles in the black,
we glanced & hurried on. But what glanced back?

The Mechanism

It lay beneath the waves uncounted years,
Survival of a shipwreck sunk in sand
Past recognition; cranks & dials & gears
Disguised by time's blind mercy. What lost hand
Contrived it—for what end—we never learned
Until too late, when apish impulse spurred
Its reconstruction. Shining sprockets turned
Inside a case of glass & brass as words
In writhing script appeared on certain plates
Installed quite blank, but speckled now with stars
Of nameless constellations. Sensing fate
Like venom in our veins, we fled—yet far
Behind us we still heard that awful whirring,
& in the void beyond, a Presence stirring.

Last Ascent

Among the rubble that a jungle makes
of man & his ambitions, tumbled stones
marked out the mercy rendered by a quake
that shattered earth & sky & blood & bone
alike: a pyramid of sacrifice
surrendered to its dark gods in a trice.

Its stairs worn concave by unwilling feet
still bore the chronicles of wizard-kings
long nameless. Tainted. Even in defeat --
writ *death*—such wisdom wrought a reckoning
upon some future generation, paid
by those too ignorant to be afraid.

Their first discoverer knew little more
than grasping after wonders. Scholarship
soon paled to acquisition as the lore
of centuries fell silent in his grip
that stacked & packed, but never even tried
to crack these shadowed glyphs before he died.

Catalogued, forgotten, locked away
from lesser intellectuals who might
aspire to curiosity, they stayed
as safe as terrors may. Yet elder Night
still thirsted after what it once received
upon those sanguine steps when men believed.

In whispers slipped between the ribs of dreams
that starving scholars pray for (unaware
the void may answer), it deployed its scheme
against our world. Ambition's twisted snare
soon settled on an epigraphic dunce
who seized his opportunity at once.

No mortal mind still living held the key
to those inscriptions, until midnight brought
strange inspiration. Though ability
had hobbled him for decades, he forgot
frustration in translating, without flaw,
this fatal fracturing of cosmic law.

Soon words alone did not suffice. To raise
the thing itself became his single goal
& full-time occupation. As each day
disclosed the next, he barely felt his soul's
blood mingling with the mortar to attract
the awful Patron of this artifact.

At last, as final risers clawed against
a sky too small & clean to comprehend
their heresies, he shivered with a sense
of something waiting. *Someone.* To defend
his life seemed less than futile. Stair by stair,
he rose into the ravening dark air.

The Outlier

Few tourists linger here on afternoons
when storm clouds mark the flawless turquoise sky
with premonitions, & a raven's cry
transforms these ruins. Rutted by monsoons
past counting, still the Great North Road rolls on
from haunted Chaco, throws this distant place
into its shadow. Relic of a race
no ranger speaks of, shattered sigil drawn
too late, its first foundations twist beneath
unwary feet like serpents. Thunder comes
to waken ancient memory of drums
that filled the kivas, rattled bones & teeth
& fragile pots to sherds—but could not turn
what crawled along that road when black stars burned.

Stone Tongue

Skull curve of stone fills slow with first light. Desert varnish surrenders its scars: spiral shield warrior, five-legged crawler. Impossible antennae stab at the sun & are gone into bright hot silence.

No language this deep in the canyon. No writing. Illiteracy is safety so long as there are no shadows.

So long as night does not release these speaking wounds.

moonless
how the wind twists
between stars

Tidal Disruption Event

A star's death is most beautiful of all
The random cataclysms we embrace
Inside our darkness. Lost beyond recall

As fire drawn into filament, it falls
For gravity with cinematic grace:
A star's death. Is *most beautiful of all*

Not epitaph enough? What else to call
A sun struck down, spun out across the face
Of starving darkness? Lost beyond recall,

Its X-ray flare alerts no rescue. Mauled
By tidal claws, to die alone in space . . .
A star's death is most beautiful? Of all

Unfeeling observations, this seems small
At light-years' distance. Hardly a disgrace—
Inside our darkness, lost beyond recall,

So many inhumanities appall
Us briefly. Let this latest find its place.
A star's death is most beautiful of all
Inside our darkness, lost beyond recall.

In Our Last Darkness

In our last darkness, the stars are lonely
as air unfettered by exhalations
of grieved meat seeking a clean & vacant
grave. In vain. No aspiring survivors
rewriting the cosmos: mythology
made campfire tales for banishing shadows
from shattered minds. No final scientists
parroting some equation that promised --
maybe—alien civilizations
avid to save us. No solitary
gazer's failing vision. Just innocent
violent furnaces scattered across
the clarity of post-apocalypse
midnight, shimmering only for themselves.

Unquiet Stars

for the *Voyagers* past heliopause

We've broken through. Not once, but twice. Our shell
of solar innocence is cracked at last
& leaking ignorance into that vast
black speculation. Whether funeral knell
or triumph follows, surely letting well
enough alone was preferable, but past
all human inclination. Voyage fast
& far & often—that's what legends tell
on every shoreline. Should these cosmic sands
sing otherwise? Yet this is not our womb's
warm amniotic plasma, placid pond
for splashing in: these shadowed seas demand
a subtlety too alien. Presume
on silence through unquiet stars beyond.

Acknowledgments

Many thanks to the editors of the following publications in which the following poems first appeared:

Abyss & Apex: "Apocalypse Swap," "A City Built On Bones," "Distant Deaths of Galaxies," and "In SETI Silence"

Crypt of Cthulhu: "Stranger Tides"

Cyaegha: "Deep Winter Skies"

Dreams and Nightmares: "Stone Ghosts"

Eye to the Telescope: ""Death Spiral, Korolev Crater," New World Haunting," and "Two Meetings"

Halloween Howlings, ed. Steve Lines (Rainfall Books, 2015): "Toward Samhain"

Heroic Fantasy Quarterly: "Children of the Stone"

HWA Poetry Showcase: "The Dead in Spring," "In Our Last Darkness," and "Salisbury Twilight"

Mark of the Beast, ed. Scott David Aniolowski (Chaosium, 2016): "The Vestals"

Scifaikuest: "Blue Suns"

Spectral Realms: "All Masks are Mirrors," "Corridors Enough," "The Dark Reclaims Us," "Final Library," "The Final Turn," "Last Ascent," "Lightless Oceans," "Missed Horizons," "The Moon-Gate," "Solving For X," "Temple of the Condor," "Temple of the Plumed Serpent," "The Thirst of Sekhmet," and "Volunteers"

*Star*Line:* "Entropic," "Ghost Dunes," "Goldilocks Stars," "Tidal Disruption Event," and "Under the Plumed Serpent's Temple"

A Walk on the Weird Side, ed. Joseph S. Pulver, Sr. (NecronomiCon Providence, 2017): "Haunted Innsmouth" and "Tomb-Feasters"

Weirdbook: "The City in the Sands"

Weirdbook Annual: "A Wizard's Daughter"

Weird Fiction Review: "The Language of Forgotten Gods," "Last Justice," The Mechanism," "Mercurial Musings," and "The Outlier"

"Dark Hearts," *Faces From the House of Pain* sequence, "Midnight In the Hot Zone," "Past Equinox," "Pink Crosses," "Sepulcher of Saints," "Snatching Shadows," "Star-Tide," "Stone Tongue," "Unquiet Stars" and "Victrola (At the End of the World)" appear here for the first time.

About the Author

Ann K. Schwader is a Wyoming native currently living and writing in suburban Colorado. Her poems have appeared in publications as varied as *Weird Tales, Star*Line, Abyss & Apex, Dreams and Nightmares, Weird Fiction Review, Spectral Realms, The Heron's Nest, Modern Haiku,* and *Frogpond.*

She is the author of eight previous poetry collections and chapbooks, including *Werewoman* (Nocturnal Publications, 1990), *The Weird Sonneteers* (with Keith Allen Daniels and Jerry H. Jenkins; Anamnesis Press, 2000), *The Worms Remember* (Hive Press, 2001), *Architectures of Night* (Dark Regions, 2003), *In the Yaddith Time* (Mythos Books, 2007), *Wild Hunt of the Stars* (Sam's Dot, 2010), *Twisted in Dream: The Collected Weird Poetry of Ann K. Schwader* (Hippocampus Press, 2011), and *Dark Energies* (P'rea Press, 2015).

Schwader is a two-time Bram Stoker Award Finalist (for *Wild Hunt of the Stars* and *Dark Energies*), and has also received the Science Fiction & Fantasy Poetry Association's Rhysling Award for both short and long form verse. She was voted an SFPA Grand Master in 2018.

About the Artist

Skinny Gaviar is a visual artist, born and raised in Russia. He describes himself as a "con artist," for without Photoshop he can barely draw a stick person. Yet, a combination of photography and digital manipulation results in one-of-a-kind moderately surreal, fully robust imagery that you might have seen in past-life childhood nightmares you've forgotten all about. **skinnygaviar.com**

www.ingramcontent.com/pod-product-compliance
Lightning Source LLC
LaVergne TN
LVHW010107110826
845155LV00028B/519

* 9 7 8 1 8 8 8 9 9 3 4 7 9 *